Dear Parents:

Congratulations! Your child is taking the first steps on an exciting journey. The destination? Independent reading!

STEP INTO READING® will help your child get there. The program offers five steps to reading success. Each step includes fun stories and colorful art or photographs. In addition to original fiction and books with favorite characters, there are Step into Reading Non-Fiction Readers, Phonics Readers and Boxed Sets, Sticker Readers, and Comic Readers—a complete literacy program with something to interest every child.

Learning to Read, Step by Step!

Ready to Read   Preschool–Kindergarten
• big type and easy words • rhyme and rhythm • picture clues
For children who know the alphabet and are eager to begin reading.

Reading with Help   Preschool–Grade 1
• basic vocabulary • short sentences • simple stories
For children who recognize familiar words and sound out new words with help.

Reading on Your Own   Grades 1–3
• engaging characters • easy-to-follow plots • popular topics
For children who are ready to read on their own.

Reading Paragraphs   Grades 2–3
• challenging vocabulary • short paragraphs • exciting stories
For newly independent readers who read simple sentences with confidence.

Ready for Chapters   Grades 2–4
• chapters • longer paragraphs • full-color art
For children who want to take the plunge into chapter books but still like colorful pictures.

STEP INTO READING® is designed to give every child a successful reading experience. The grade levels are only guides; children will progress through the steps at their own speed, developing confidence in their reading.

Remember, a lifetime love of reading starts with a single step!

To all the brave girls
who fight for freedom
—T.L.

All rights reserved. Published in the United States by Random House Children's Books, a division of Penguin Random House LLC, 1745 Broadway, New York, NY 10019, and in Canada by Penguin Random House Canada Limited, Toronto.

Step into Reading, Random House, and the Random House colophon are registered trademarks of Penguin Random House LLC.

Visit us on the web!
StepIntoReading.com
rhcbooks.com

Educators and librarians, for a variety of teaching tools, visit us at RHTeachersLibrarians.com

ISBN 978-0-593-38191-5 (trade) — ISBN 978-0-593-38192-2 (lib. bdg.)
ISBN 978-0-593-38193-9 (ebook)

Printed in the United States of America
10 9 8 7 6 5 4 3 2 1

☆ American Girl®

Freedom for Addy

by Tonya Leslie

illustrated by Tanisha Cherislin

Random House 🏠 New York

It is 1864, during the Civil War.
Addy and her family live on
a plantation in North Carolina.
They are enslaved
and considered property.
They work all day.
They do not get paid.
It's a hard life.

At bedtime, Addy, brother Sam,
and baby Esther sleep
on the floor of their small cabin.
Addy hears Momma and Poppa
whisper in the dark about
freedom . . . and running away.
Addy listens and wonders
what will happen.
Escape attempts are punished.

The next day, Addy hears
the plantation owner talking.
He says Sam and Poppa
are going to be sold.
Addy's family will be separated!
She rushes to warn them.

Addy almost spills the water
in her hurry to reach them.
"Girl," the owner yells.
"Watch yourself."
He heads to the field.
Addy's heart races with fear.

Addy is too late!

Poppa and Sam are being loaded

onto a wagon.

Their hands are bound.

Addy drops the bucket.

She runs to them,

but the owner stops her.

He shoves her back.

Addy falls into her mother's arms.

"Stop crying!" the owner growls.

"Get back to work!"

Addy's heart is breaking.

Addy and her mother
have no choice.
They must return to work.

That night, the cabin feels empty
without Poppa and Sam.
"We are not safe here,"
Momma says. "We must run!
But we can't take baby Esther."
Esther can't walk yet, and
her crying could give them away.

Addy's auntie and uncle help.

They dress Addy like a boy.

Momma is dressed like a man.

Uncle Solomon gives Addy a dime.

"Freedom's got a cost," he says.

Addy kisses baby Esther goodbye.

Momma and Addy move quickly.

They are headed north to freedom.

The forest is dark and scary.

They stumble through the trees.

After a long while, they find

a small cave to shelter in.

Addy is tired and misses her family.

Momma takes out a small shell.

"This shell belonged to your
great-grandma," says Momma.

"She brought it from Africa."

Momma puts the shell on a string
and around Addy's neck.

Addy knows she must be brave
like her great-grandma.

Addy and Momma travel by night

so they won't get caught.

One night, their path ends at a river.

They must cross it,

but Momma can't swim.

Addy and Momma get into
the cold river.
Momma slips!
Her head goes under.
Addy reaches for her
and pulls her to shore.

"You saved me, Addy,"

Momma says weakly.

"You are a brave girl."

Momma and Addy go far away,

as fast as they can. At last,

a small house comes into view.

Is it safe? They knock and wait.

A woman named Miss Caroline
invites them in
and gives them food and new clothes.
She wants them to be free.
In the morning, Addy and her momma
will have to hide in a wagon
to continue the journey to freedom.

The wagon takes them to a boat.

The boat takes them
to Philadelphia.

The big city is a sea

of strangers.

The streets are full
of people and wagons.
It's all unfamiliar.
Addy and Momma do not know
how to read the signs.
They cannot trust strangers.
They must wait for help.

New friends help them get settled.
A girl named Sarah and her mother
walk Addy and Momma
to the church for aid.

Sarah's mother helps them
find a place to live.
It is small but cozy.
Momma will have to work hard
at her new job sewing clothes,
but at least she will get paid.

One day, Addy gets good news.

She will be going to school!

She will finally learn to read!

Addy is nervous

on the first day of school.

Will she make friends?

One girl makes friends
with Addy right away.
It's Sarah, the girl Addy met
the day she arrived.

The holidays come.

Addy's momma works all the time.

Addy wants to give

her mother a gift.

She considers

using the dime from Uncle Solomon

to buy a red scarf.

Instead, she makes a scarf
with scrap fabric.
Addy gives the dime
to the church to help
other enslaved people escape.

It is Christmas Day.

Addy gives Momma

the scarf that she made.

Momma loves the present!

She has a gift for Addy, too.

It is a rag doll stuffed with beans.

"I'll call her Ida Bean," Addy says.

Later that night at church,

there is a surprise for Addy . . .

It's Poppa!

He has found them!

It's the best holiday surprise.

Addy hopes she will soon see

her brother and sister again, too.